I0517487

MELISSA BATES

THE ADVENTURES OF Lavender

MELISSA BATES

THE
ADVENTURES
OF
Lavender

United States Copyright Office
© 2019, The Adventures of Lavender
Author: Melissa Bates
mnbates2@gmail.com

Published by Anointed Fire™ House
Cover Design by Anointed Fire™ House
Website: www.anointedfirehouse.com

ALL RIGHTS RESERVED. This book contains material protected under International and Federal Copyright Laws and Treaties. Any unauthorized reprint or use of this material is prohibited. No part of this book may be reproduced or transmitted in any form or by any means, electronic or mechanical, including photocopying, recording, or by any information storage and retrieval system without express written permission from the author/publisher.

You may NOT sell or redistribute this book!

The stories in this book are fictional. Names, characters, businesses, places, events and incidents are either the products of the author's imagination or used in a fictitious manner. Any resemblance to actual persons, living or dead, or actual events is purely coincidental.

ISBN-13: 978-1-7331127-2-7

Dedication

This book is dedicated to my Lord and Savior Jesus Christ.

TABLE OF CONTENTS

Introduction...IX

Chapter 1...

Dry Bones...1

Chapter 2...

Life-Giving Aroma.................................15

Chapter 3...

Lavender, the Cat.................................25

Chapter 4...

Time of Testing.................................45

Chapter 5...

Saved...65

Chapter 6...

In the Spring Time.................................83

Chapter 7...

Rest...93

Chapter 8...

I Can See...103

Chapter 9...

Growth and Journey.................................117

Chapter 10...

Raised to Life...127

Introduction

It's common nowadays to not read the Bible. In today's culture, being passionate about reading the Bible is not a cool thing to do. This book will change that notion. The purpose of this fictional novel is to produce a hunger and a genuine curiosity for reading the Bible. It is a book that can change your life, and with the help of the Holy Spirit, your life will be transformed. I want to encourage every reader to use their imagination when reading the Bible. Why? Because if you dwell on how someone was feeling in a situation, you can better relate and learn from them. For example, in the Book of Psalms, David wrote a lot about how sad and hopeless he felt, yet, he chose to trust in the Lord (Psalm 27:13-14). When you read the various stories of the Bible, see the people as living creatures and try to relate to them, you will be in a position to learn from them and comprehend the Bible better. You can do this by finding something that you have in common. Become interested in reading the Bible. The goal of this is to learn from their trials and circumstances. Think of it as a guide to your life.

The Bible is a fascinating book; it was written by men who were guided by the Holy Spirit. The Bible is alive because it is constantly speaking. One verse can give you revelation for years to come. One passage may stick with you and guide you through a hard time.

Have you ever read the Bible and wondered what you would have done if you had been there, experiencing many of the wonderful situations that the men and women of old experienced? I wonder how so-and-so felt when that happened. Well, in this fictional story, use your imagination and think about what you would do if you could see into the Bible with the help of the Holy Spirit. Think about how experiencing the Bible in a tangible way would change you. Would you get closer to God or would you run away because of fear? How would you feel if you spoke with the people in the Bible? Would you remain the same or would you be changed? Take a walk in the shoes of a fictional character named Nicole as she discovers the Bible like never before.

Chapter 1

DRY BONES

It was an unusually cold day, even though the
sun was bright and no clouds were in the sky. I
looked up at the pale blue sky. It was calming,
and the cool air felt comforting. My favorite
time of year is Autumn in Texas. The sky
seems larger and the crisp air is refreshing; it
feels as though it can cleanse my lungs. I
glanced up at the sky one more time before
heading into work, the bane of my existence. I
had been an assistant manager at Stacie Pearl
for about two years. I got this job after the start-
up company I was working for went belly up. I
remember how strange my interview was for
this job. Before applying for the position, I never shopped or worked at a high-end clothing
boutique. Since I had no point of reference, I
was surprised when I received a call to come in
for an interview. I came in thinking I was just
going to ring up customers and fold sweaters,
however, I was highly mistaken. My interview
was with a woman who referred to herself as
Diva. She told me that she was a stylist to the

1

stars and how they had her on speed dial because she was very gifted at styling outfits. After the interview which, by the way, was mostly
about her career and life story, she adjusted
her diamond-studded glasses and looked me
up and down. "So, when can you start?" I was
taken aback by the sudden question, so after a
long and awkward stare, I said, "Tomorrow?"
Two years after the interview, I was still at Stacie Pearl. I took a deep sigh and got out of my
car. A cold gust of wind hit me, so I tightened
my trench coat's belt and crossed my arms. After two years of working as an assistant manager, I have learned how to forsake comfort for
the sake of fashion. The store manager has
drilled into all the employees' minds that we are
walking mannequins and we must wear the latest fashions of Stacie Pearl. One day, she even
told us, "If you want to be successful, you must
eat, drink and sleep Stacie Pearl!" It sounds
appealing at first, but wearing heels and dressing up gets old real fast. I always looked forward to wearing joggers and sneakers on my

off days. I glanced down at my black leather boots and bent over to rub off a scuff mark. I didn't want to hear Diva complaining about how I was not representing Stacie Pearl properly by wearing scuffed boots. I stood back up to lean on my car. The parking lot was crowded, and people were buzzing in and out of stores. I took one more deep breath of the fresh Fall air and exhaled. It was Black Friday and I just wanted to go home.

The store was in complete chaos when I walked in. Once a year, Stacie Pearl has a sale and it's huge. Everything is 65% off, from cashmere sweat pants to alligator trimmed peacoats. The store's normal hours are from 10 am to 5 pm, but on Black Friday, we are open from 6 am to 10 pm. I'm not a morning person, so I was a little bit grateful that my shift was from 1 pm to 10 pm. As soon as I walked in the door, I was met with absolute pandemonium. The mannequins were stripped bare, women were scurrying back and forth with racks of clothes in their arms and the checkout line was zig-zagging throughout the whole store.

I made my way towards the back of the store so I could put my purse in the back office. That's when Diva popped out from the stock-room. "Nicole, we need all hands-on deck. I need you at the cash wrap stat!" Before she could even turn to finish whatever else she was doing, a customer scurried up to her with an armful of shoes and asked, "Do you have these in a size six?" I laughed to myself at the sight of Diva being overwhelmed by customers. It serves her right. She was always so quick to boss us around; I was glad a customer was giving her a piece of her own medicine. Once I made it to the back office, I put my stuff away and checked my makeup and clothes. I wanted to make sure I was adhering to the Stacie Pearl dress code. I immediately made a bee-line to the cash wrap while simultaneously try-ing to dodge the customers running back and forth from the fitting rooms with racks of clothes. I barely got a chance to say hi to my coworkers before someone dropped a mile-high pile of clothes on the counter and demanded to know how much they cost. We have an inside joke at Stacie Pearl about holiday customers. We say they come out once a year to wreak havoc on unsuspecting retail employees. That year's crowd had yet to disappoint. "I can help the next in line!" A frazzled older woman walked up to the register and I said, "Hi, what can I help you wi….?" Before I could finish what I was saying, she dumped a package on the counter and said, "I have a return." That was it; I wanted to scream! Who comes into a store to return items on Black Friday?! It seemed as if everyone in the ever-growing line frowned as soon as she said return. Even my co-workers glanced over to see if this customer was serious. I had to blink a couple of times to regain my composure after the initial shock of her request. Thankfully, I have mastered the art of becoming a walking and talking robot for Stacie Pearl, so I faked a smile, looked the customer straight in the eye and said, "Sure, I can do that for you."

The sky is pale blue, no clouds as far as the eye can see. If not for the cold air, I would think it was Summer. The autumn season in Texas is deceitful; from the view out my window, it looks like a warm sunny day. However, once I walk outside, I can feel that it's cold. When I sit out on the patio, I can feel the dryness in the air. I like to look out towards the park in the distance and see the colorful leaves twirl around as the wind whips through the trees. Autumn is a transitional time, the last speck of life before Winter takes over and everything hides or dies.

This is how I feel; I am dry in my spirit. My inner man feels like a dry dull autumn day. The deceitful Texas weather is reflecting the state of my heart. If you were to look at the outward appearance, everything would appear good— my clothes are high-end and high quality. My default face is a slight smile. My life looks fine. My outward appearance is alright by the world's standards, but a closer look with a well-discerning eye would reveal that I am a changing season. I'm a deceiving Fall day. The light is slowly fading, and darkness is inching closer. The warm air is gone and cooler air is coming. I feel like I am becoming more indifferent. I just don't care about anything anymore. I have no passions or desires. I feel dispirited. It reminds me of the Bible verse John 12:35, which reads, "Light is still apparent, but the darkness seeks to overtake it." The light is the knowledge that I am becoming more and more apathetic. It's like autumn in my heart. If this indifference continues, coldness will enter my heart. Darkness will creep in slowly, and before I realize it, Winter will consume me. The season of Winter is cold and stagnant. My hope and desires will curl up and hibernate. My aspirations and dreams will mourn for the light of day. I don't want my heart to become cold and indifferent. I don't want to appear to be bright and sunny, with no productivity or growth, just deceitful stagnation—the illusion of Summer until you look for life. How disheartening it is to think it's Summer and to expect warmth, only to be met with bitter frigid air—wind that chills your spine and shocks your lungs. Lord, I don't want to live like this. Why am I so empty?

Journal Entry: 11/19/2018

I am not sure when the coldness started to creep in. All I know is I feel emotionally numb. My life has become an uneventful cycle, whereas I wake up, eat, work, sleep and then repeat. I feel disinterested in everything. I know this can't be good. Lord, help me to feel again; this place I am in is not for a child of God. This feeling is confusing. I am disheartened by the fact that I need to keep on reminding myself that I can't become detached and stagnant. Why am I so prone to these emotions? It's as if apathy and indifference are my default moods. Why should a child of God be dry and empty? If I am connected to the Life Giver, shouldn't I be a bright and shiny example of life to the world? I need a serious overhaul, I need a total renovation, I need to master this thing on the inside of me. I have managed to master the outward part of me. I got braces to fix my teeth, I exercised to lose weight, I followed a hair care regimen to grow my hair, and I eat healthy. I even work at a high-end clothing store to get discounts so I can have nice clothes. Maybe I have become an anomaly, a real-life mannequin. I look seemingly perfect, yet, I am completely empty inside. I feel as though I've mastered the whole outward appearance thing, but it's pointless; it's vanity upon vanity. I can't even recall what my dreams were from years ago. What are my dreams? What are my desires? Well, I did want to get married and have a bunch of children, but I gave up trying to get married three years ago. I felt like to get married, I needed a secret password that everybody knew but me. All of my serious boyfriends got married six months after breaking up with me. After the fifth wedding of an ex-boyfriend, I was too offended to cry. I just gave up on marriage. I used to say to myself that I'm smart, pretty, have nice teeth and love Jesus, and yet, no one is seriously pursuing me. What's the deal? Even my two closest friends have yet to decode the secret of marriage. Andrea is a talented clothing designer; she can do anything and look fabulous doing it, yet, all her suitors flee after 30 days. Sasha is a beautiful and smart nurse with the body of a supermodel, and her last relationship ended in a "it's not you, it's me" speech.

Why do I feel so empty as a Christian? Don't I possess a treasure? I am reminded of the verse that says, "The kingdom of heaven is like a treasure hidden in the field, which a man found and hid again; and from joy over it he goes and sells all that he has and buys that field" (Matthew 13:44-46). In the church, I remember reading John 14:26, which reads, "The Helper will teach you all things and bring to your remembrance all that I have said to you." So, my helper is the Holy Spirit. Well Helper, can you help me? I feel so dry and humdrum. What's the use? I don't even know the Holy Spirit. I don't even think I understand what He does and how to get to know the Holy Spirit. I understand the words in theory. I can even repeat them and say words that seem like I know what I am talking about, but I don't have experimental knowledge on the subject. I haven't knowingly experienced the Holy Spirit in a tangible way.

"Urggh I am so over these Black Friday Shoppers," said Natalie, a Junior at Southern Methodist University. She's a sweet girl who would always help during the holidays. She had an edgy but conservative style, so Diva didn't nag her about dressing the part of a Stacie Pearl Fashion Ambassador. Lately, she had been experimenting with rose gold hair and bangs. Her thin frame, high pitched voice, and colored hair made her look like a fairy.

"Same here!"Juana chimed in. Juana was a book-loving introvert with a love for the color black. Juana worked at Stacie Pearl part-time. She worked full time as a receptionist at a nearby hospital. She angrily picked up a few cashmere sweaters off the floor of the fitting rooms. "These Black Friday customers are the worst kind of people! They have no respect for my precious cashmere!" Both Natalie and I burst out laughing; we had never heard Juana vent so passionately about anything. I helped fold the sweaters and hung up dresses. Juana and Natalie are the only reason my job is bearable. They keep me laughing.

Natalie: Oh, yea—speaking of disrespectful. Can you believe that lady wanted to return some pants on Black Friday? As soon as she said return, everyone just glared at her.
Juana: If looks could kill.
Nicole: She was so frazzled and eager to return those pants, I was confused. Maybe she thought it was a normal Friday.

Juana: Normal Friday my foot! Who could over-look people turning into beasts over a sixty-five percent off sale?

I looked down to pick up a trampled scarf and saw a flyer underneath the tables where the silk scarves had been displayed. I skimmed over it curiously before shouting to my two co-workers. "Hey, did you know the Dallas Animal Shelter is having a Black Friday pop-up pet adoptions' event? It ends this Saturday. I have been thinking about getting a cat." "Ohhhhh really?!" squealed Natalie. "I wonder if my mom will let me buy a puppy for my little brother." Juana: "I have never heard of Black Friday specials for pet adoptions. What if they are crazy or not even pets?
Nicole: Not even pets?! I'll keep an eye out for opossums with cat-ear headbands on.
Juana: So, when are you going to buy this mythical creature?
Nicole: I think I'll go tomorrow. I'm off Saturday.

Juana and Natalie: What!? You're off tomorrow?!

Natalie: The Diva didn't schedule you to work on a Saturday?

Juana: How did you manage that?

Nicole: It's a miracle, I guess.

Chapter 2

LIFE-GIVING AROMA

Tick tick tick, beep beep beep beep. "Urghh! Why is this on?! It's my off day!" I grumbled quietly as I stretched my hand from under the blanket. I peeked out from under the covers to make sure I didn't knock over anything on my side table while I turned off my alarm clock. After I turned off the alarm clock, I put the covers back over my head to go back to sleep. As I was dozing off, I could smell fruits. It was like fresh fruit juice—a sweet fragrance of pineapple, cherries and citrus aromas. I remember thinking how I liked the smell right before I went back to sleep.

Around 11 that morning, I slowly rolled out of bed. I walked to the bathroom and started to think about where the fruity fragrance was coming from. I looked over at my trays of body washes, soaps and skincare products that I kept on the counter-top. "Maybe, I have too many scented products since I can smell them all the way in my bedroom. I'll have to organize all of this later," I said to myself. I stood in the mirror brushing my teeth. My mind wandered back to how empty I felt. I started to think about how all the skincare products, clothes, and accessories were a poor attempt of mine at finding fulfillment.

Once I finished brushing my teeth and washing my face, I stared into the mirror at my reflection. I then spoke to myself. "Nicole, you're a thirty-year-old woman with no kids or husband. You hate your job, but you stay because you like the generous 75% off employee discount. You don't have any genuine friends, just random acquaintances that you have light conversations with. What happened to you? You used to be so full of life and you used to be passionate about your dreams. Now, you've become like an empty shell. You're just like a mannequin—trendy, yet, empty. Lord, help me."

After my depressing pep talk, I got dressed in my usual get-up of the latest Stacie Pearl collections. I then poured some Oolong tea in my travel mug and headed out the door to adopt a cat. I typed in the directions from the flyer into Google Maps. I noticed that the Dallas Animal Shelter was sponsoring the pop-up event only five minutes away from my house. I pulled into a small plaza where the pop-up shop was located. The parking lot was unexpectedly empty for a Black Friday weekend. The plaza was a new construction and most of the storefronts had not been leased yet. I walked up to the pop-up shop and opened the door. I was met with the same citrus aroma I'd smelled at home. The store was very bright and clean. I thought to myself that the place was too clean and smelled too fresh to have cats and dogs in it. I looked around to see if anyone was working. I wanted to ask about the special rates they were having on pet adoptions. The store was small; I could see all the way to the back from the front door. An older man holding a bag of dog food entered from a door near the back and greeted me. He was wearing a white t-shirt, white jeans and a white apron. He had a very pleasant demeanor. He seemed like a man who lived a peaceful life. As he got closer to me, I noticed he had very nice skin and he was extremely radiant. I thought to myself, "Is he wearing highlighter?"

"Hi, you must be here for our Black Friday pet special. My name's Wyatt, by the way. Nice to meet you." He eagerly extended his hand to shake mine.

"Hi, I'm Nicole nice to meet you too."

"I'll show you where the cats are."

"How did you know I wanted a cat?"

"I had a hunch that a cat was what you were looking for."

He opened the door to reveal a large bright white room. There were 15 cages in total and all the doors to the cages were open. The animals were either sleeping or eating. They were very quiet. I was impressed by the facility. It was very clean and smelled like fruits and citrus. This place was heaven compared to the animal shelters I had visited in the past. I was also shocked at how well behaved all the cats were. There was no meowing; they were hanging out like nothing was going on.

The first thing I noticed in the cat room were the cute kittens walking around. I wanted an older cat because I was busy working and didn't have time to take care of a kitten. However, they were so adorable that it was hard to resist not getting one.

Most of what I saw were kittens playing or sleeping in curled up balls. There was a random dog as well. I watched the small puppy sloppily lap up water while wagging his tail. "Oh, he's a cute puppy! He is so small I almost mistook him for a cat."
"That's Charlie. He likes to hang out with the cats. We have an open cage policy here so the animals can roam around if they want."
While Wyatt was bending down and petting Charlie, I looked around at the cats to see which one I wanted to adopt.

Whoa! I gasped as I walked past one cat.

"Yeah, that's Crazy Eyes. He's a good boy, it's just that he has an intimating gaze."

"Crazy eyes, indeed."

I cautiously walked past him as he glared at me. He was a large, long-haired black and white male cat with eyes like an owl. Plus, the way his fur grew around his eyes made him look as if he was frowning. I walked around petting and looking at all the cats before I ended up at the very last cage on the bottom. I peered into the cage and saw a small, short--haired black cat. She looked up at me and softly meowed.

"Hi, kitty! Were you sleeping?"

"Oh, that's Lavender; she's real sweet."

"How old is she?"

"She's old enough to get adopted. Just know that she is a healthy gal with a good disposition."

"She looks small, though. Is she fully grown?"

"Yeah, that's probably as big as she's going to get. My guess is she was the runt of the litter.

Do you want me to coax her out the cage so you can pet her?

"Yes, please."

Wyatt grabbed some cat treats and sprinkled a few of them on the floor. Lavender perked up and cautiously walked out of her cage so that she could eat her snacks. I scratched behind her ears as she purred and rubbed against my boots.

"Okay, I'm sold. She is the one I am adopting."

"Congratulations, she's free!"

"Really? There is no adoption fee?"

"Yep, that was part of our promotion, the special Black Friday deal. One of our pets up for adoption was free."

I picked up Lavender, and she began to purr and sway her tail.

"Well, thank you!" I said. "This was a complete surprise. I need to buy some cat supplies too. Can you help me pick out some things for her? Wyatt happily agreed. "I sure can!" he said.

Chapter 3

LAVENDER, THE CAT

Journal Entry 12/3/2018

It's been exactly ten days since I got Lavender. She is a very calm cat. I took her to the vet recently to make sure she is healthy and caught up with her shots. Apparently, she is seven years old and in great health. I feel like she could gain a few more pounds so I have been keeping her bowl filled with wet cat food and treats. Lavender has such a peaceful demeanor. I jokingly call her the chill cat. She likes to lay in the window in the morning and bask in the sun. At night, she curls up in a ball at the edge of my bed, or sometimes, she sits on the rug in my bedroom. Having a cat in my house is nice and my attitude is better. God had to have created certain animals to be companions because my mood is better just by having a cat around to be responsible for. She's nothing like how she was at the pop-up shop. She is very vocal when I say, "Hey Vendy" She'll meow back. It's as if she is saying, "What!?" If I am on the phone, she sits near me as if she is eavesdropping on my conversations. She likes to lounge and hang around me, and it makes me feel better. I still feel empty, but having Lavender around makes me feel a little more upbeat. The responsibility of a pet does help me feel less empty in life. I can understand why pets are companions, and that is something to be grateful for.

The next day when I went to work, I noticed that everyone was whispering and chattering among themselves. I asked Allison (one of the stock room workers) about their odd behavior; this was while I was in the stock room looking for a shirt for a customer.

"Hey, what's going on? Everyone is whispering, but I'm so busy with helping customers that I didn't get a chance to ask."

Allison responded, "You didn't hear? Cheryl confronted Diva about her attitude, how rude she is to all of us and how she makes this working place horrible. Diva fired her. Can you believe that?" I was in shock. "What?! Why would she fire Cheryl?" I asked. "Cheryl's been here longer than all of us. She knows all the names of our frequent customers, and she never forgets our birthdays. This really sucks. Suddenly, there was a knock on the door. Allison looked around and asked, "Who's that knocking on the stock room door?" I signed, "I came back here to get a shirt for a customer. I bet you that's her knocking." Allison rolled her eyes. "Urghh! Holiday shoppers are the worst."

Journal Entry 12/15/2018

Lavender helps me calm down after work. This week has been crazy dealing with Diva, holiday shoppers and the drama that comes with a store full of women. Today, I heard that Diva had a complete meltdown and fired one of our best associates. Cheryl was everyone's favorite. She was the sweetest woman anyone could meet. The customers loved her and all the Stacy Pearl associates loved her too. Everyone enjoyed Cheryl's company except our

*crazy store manager, Diva. At times like these,
I wish I could give her a piece of my mind.*

For the next two weeks, the store stayed open
for an extra four hours to accommodate the
Christmas shoppers. Additionally, every night
that week, we had about two or three customers who wanted to stay past closing.

It had been a long day at Stacie Pearl. Juana
and I were the only ones working that night. I'd
let Natalie go home early because she wasn't
feeling well. I think the combination of cold air
and needy customers would make anyone
sick. My coworkers and I hate when customers
stay past closing because that means we can't
go home until they leave. Around this time of
the year, we always get straggler shoppers
who stay past closing. Once I start closing the
registers, they usually get the hint to leave.
Juana and I jokingly call this behavior passive
harassment. On nights like those, I wish I could
make a public service announcement and tell

the world that if the store is closed, please don't stick around; we can't go home until you go home!

Juana nudged me and whispered, "It's 10:05 pm. I will not be harassed anymore. These lingering shoppers have got to go." I looked around. "I'm closing the registers," I said. "Once they are closed, everyone is leaving." Juana looked at me, and as serious as she looked, I knew she was just frustrated. "I'm only sticking around for the Spring collection and then, I'm out of here," she said pursing her lips together. I laughed."You said that about the Fall season too. This store is a trap; they keep us here with the good discount. Can you believe my entire wardrobe is from Stacie Pearl? Even my socks come from here."Juana couldn't resist laughing."You're right," she said sheepishly. "I'm just working for clothes. I even bought the silk joggers. I couldn't resist."
I paused for a minute to think about the pants she'd worn."Ooh yeah," I said as I opened the

register. "Those were some cute pants too. I bought the cashmere joggers last season. I do agree with you about working for clothes. I believe everyone except Diva works here because of the clothes. Do you think we have a shopping problem?" We both looked at one another and said in unison, "Nope!" After this, we quietly joked some more while I finished closing the registers.

Thankfully, the drive to work is a short eight-minute commute. Typically, around this time of year, I close the store often so that means I get home around 10:30 pm. On that night when I got home, I was mentally and physically drained. I called Cheryl on my way home just to tell her how much the girls missed her and that we should catch up over brunch someday. The short conversation I had with her made me a little sad. Sometimes, it seems like the good guys never win and the bad guys always prevail.

Journal Entry 12/23/2108

*I was frustrated today with my working situa-
tion and I felt hopeless regarding my dreams
and aspirations. At this point, I feel like I only
work for clothes. I have no passion for this job.
I just like what I can get from it. Stacie Pearl
has good benefits for employees, and there
are also a lot of perks to this job. This season,
we had vouchers that included two sweaters
for free. We also received two vouchers for a
"buy one, get one free" offer on top of our sev-
enty percent off. The vouchers and employee
discount are generous, and because of this,
my entire wardrobe is nice, but at what cost? I
hate my job! I feel drained, I feel empty, and I
feel like I really don't have a purpose in life. My
life has become a cycle of retail so much so
that I even think of my life in seasons. Spring
collection, Summer collection, Fall collection,
and Winter collection is what my life revolves
around. The only thing that changes about me
is my wardrobe. I still feel depressed, frustrated, hollow, and hopeless. I don't have anyone*

to come home to, only Lavender, but I still feel empty. The friendships I make with the customers feel superficial. It's as if I am a cyborg that smiles and greets customers. They come in and I give them pleasant small talk to make their shopping experience nice, but I don't care about anything they are saying.

Journal Entry 12/24/2018

It finally feels like Winter. This week has been freezing cold, and my demeanor matches it. It's Christmas Eve and I am at home being a grouch. Two people from work invited me to a Christmas party and I declined. I have no desire to hang out or chat it up. I think I might be depressed. When was the last time I went to church? Maybe, it was in November. Work has been so hectic that I haven't been to church in a while, even though I have Sundays off. I made a point to request Sundays off so there's no reason why I shouldn't be attending church. The last time I read my Bible, I was in First Timothy. I read about a paragraph and then, fell asleep. I am going to start reading my Bible again. That's probably the main reason why I feel so empty and depressed. For someone who has been raised in a Christian home, I really don't know much about the Bible or how to use it as a guide to life. I suppose reading it would help me get a clue about how to live well. I can almost hear my parents nagging me, "It's because you don't go to church or read your Bible. Of course, you will fill empty if you just go through life like that."

I closed my journal and placed it on the nightstand next to my bed. Lavender was curled up in a ball on the ottoman by my bed. I looked over at her to see if she was sleeping. "Hey Vendy, you sleep? She perked her head up and meowed softly. "I'm going to start reading my Bible; you want to join me?" Lavender got up, did some cat stretches and hopped onto the bed. "I suppose you approve of me getting my life together, huh?" Lavender looked at me and meowed again. "Exactly! That's what I thought. It is a good idea. This will probably help me feel better; don't you think?" Lavender looked towards me and softly meowed. "See, we're on the same page. That's why I like you Vendy; we understand each other perfectly."

I got up and dug through my closet to find my Bible. I sat back on my bed and grabbed my phone to google passages about the Holy Spirit. The Holy Spirit seems like a very interesting topic to study. I don't think I know what it is. I thought about this subject before, and it left me stumped. It's not like I'm new to Christianity. I went to Bible study as a kid and grew up going to church; that was the norm for my family. When I was older, I would go and sit in the sanctuary and listen to the sermons. I even got to the point where I would take notes so that I could try to apply what our pastor preached about in my everyday life. Some of the things he taught seemed impossible to master because they were not humanly possible in my opinion. For example, the whole love one another command was hard for me to grasp. I could understand the idea of loving people who were kind to me, but to love people who persecute me—how is that possible? To accomplish this feat, would sincerely require some sort of supernatural power.

"Here's a good verse I can read," I mumbled to myself as I opened my Bible and turned to John 15 :26. It reads, "When the advocate comes whom I will send to you from the father the spirit of truth who goes out from the father he will testify about me and you will also testify for you have been with me from the beginning." I read this verse one more time before sighing. "What does this mean?" I skimmed over the verse again. "Now I can see why I'm confused. I should probably read the whole chapter." I remembered our pastor would tell us not to take things out of context; he'd follow this statement up with, "Read the whole thing." Perhaps, if I read the whole chapter, I would be able to understand how the Holy Spirit is my advocate. I started to read chapter 15 of the Book of John

and continued to 16. For some reason, Lavender seemed very interested in my Bible. While I sat up on my bed and read the Bible, she would come and sit right in front of me. It's as if she wanted to know what I was reading.
My eyelids were getting heavy and my head slowly tilted forward. The more I read, the drowsier I got. I shook my head to try to wake up so I could continue reading, but to no avail. I could hardly read the words on the page. I was very exhausted. I put the Bible aside and fluffed up my pillow underneath my head so I could get comfortable. I drifted off to sleep, but while I was still conscious, I heard a voice that I've never heard before. It said, "You should pray to receive the Holy Spirit." After this, I fell asleep.

The next morning, I woke up late. I'd completely forgot about the voice I'd heard until I was driving to my parents' house to celebrate Christmas with my family. "You should pray to receive the Holy Spirit." That was a weird dream and that voice was strange. I didn't understand, but decided that it was definitely a good idea to pray for the Holy Spirit. "Is the Holy Spirit something you can ask for?" I asked myself while driving. "I have never heard anyone say this before, and I've been going to church forever. When I get home, I'll look up some Bible verses about praying for the Holy Spirit," I reasoned with myself.

Christmas was just a highly decorated ordinary day for me. I visited my parents in East Texas and gave my sisters and mom clothing from Stacie Pearl. My dad and brother in-law got some tech gadgets I'd found at Best Buy. My parents' church has an annual service on Christmas day, so every year, we open presents, eat breakfast and go to 10 am Christmas service. On that day, we all went to church together, but I was not feeling it. I honestly felt bad about my attitude. I was in church and didn't feel moved at all. I was like a stone. I thought to myself, "Alright, it is Christmas, Nicole, you need to get it together." Jesus is the reason for the season, so at least fake like you're saved." After my conversation with myself, I sang along to a few church hymns and clapped to a couple of songs. After this, I zoned out for the rest of the service.

Christmas flew by and the new year was fast approaching. Work had been crazy with us setting up the new collection and revamping the store's layout for 2019. Another long day at work had left me drained and exhausted. I was greeted by Lavender as soon as I walked into the house. She has a habit of following me everywhere now. I checked to make sure she had food and water in her bowl. After that, I bent down to pet her head. I threw my purse and coat on the living room couch, kicked off my velvet boots and proceeded to lounge on my couch while I processed what I'd done that day. Lavender jumped on the armrest of the couch and meowed at me. I pet her head for a few minutes before standing to my feet. It was time for me to get ready for bed.

Before I go to sleep, I try to read my Bible. I started getting in the habit of praying also. Ever since I had the dream about praying for the Holy Spirit, I started to be more consistent with my Bible reading. What I noticed in the few days I'd been reading and praying is that reading the Bible does help me feel grounded. It's as though I have a steady place to rest my feet as I walk through life. I don't have a system for reading through the Bible, however. I typically open it up and read whatever chapter it turns to. A few times, it landed in the Book of Numbers in the chapters where there are long lists of genealogy. I skipped those sections.

One day, I wanted to read more about the Holy Spirit, so I opened the Book of John and read chapter 14. While I was reading through the text, John 14:17 stuck out to me. I had to dwell on it and reread it again. It reads, "The world is unable to receive Him because it doesn't see Him or know Him." Did that mean I belonged to the world if I didn't know Him? That portion concerned me. I wanted to know the Holy Spirit, but how? I began to recall the dream I had where I'd heard a voice telling me to pray for the Holy Spirit. I had never prayed for the Holy Spirit before.

I stared blankly as I tried to think of how to pray. Lavender seemed to notice my confusion and gently pawed at my hand so I could pet her. "Lavender, how am I supposed to pray for the Holy Spirit? Do I just ask for it? It can't possibly be that simple. Lord, can I have the Holy Spirit?" I waited a little bit and scanned my room, thinking something was supposed to happen. "Well, that wasn't the fanciest prayer, but I was sincere." One thing I did learn from church was that God hears sincere prayers. There's no point in saying fake prayers like, "Thy Father, ye of the blessed—blah blah blah." I never understood why people talked like that at church. After my simple prayer, I read my Bible some more, and as usual, I started to nod off to sleep. I put my Bible on the nightstand and turned off the nearby lamp. I laid down to fall asleep and I heard, "The Lord has answered your prayers, Nicole." I turned my head when I heard this voice. I was half asleep and assumed I was dreaming. When I opened my eyes, I saw Lavender leaning over me. I got startled by her looking at me so closely. "Lavender, why are you in front of me? I'm trying to sleep. That scared me!" I griped as I fluffed my pillow to get comfortable.

"Sorry, I didn't mean to startle you," the voice seemed to come from Lavender.

"Ahhhhh!" I screamed.

Chapter 4

TIME OF TESTING

I was so frightened, I froze. All I could do was cover my head with my blanket and cry out in my mind, "Jesus, help me," repeatedly.

"Why are you afraid? I am here to help you," the voice replied.

With a shaky voice, I whimpered, "Go away."

"I can't go away until I help you."

Still fearful of my talking cat, I stuttered, "Wha, wha—why are you ta-ta talking to me?"

"This is the only way to get your attention, so the Holy Spirit enabled me to speak so I could help you."

I peeked my head out of the blanket and looked at Lavender. She was sitting at the edge of my bed in what I call a cat loaf with her eyes somewhat closed as if she was going to sleep. Somehow, seeing her in a relaxed position made me less scared.

"So, who is making you talk to me?"

"I can speak to you by the power of the Holy Spirit."

"Oh no, you're the devil. The only talking animal that spoke to a person was a snake in the Garden of Eden."

"Don't you know the story of Balaam's Donkey?"

"Who?"

"Read the Book of Numbers, chapter 22." Lavender got up and pawed at the Bible near my nightstand. I cautiously picked up my Bible and turned to Numbers chapter 22, After this, I began to read.

While reading the passage in the Bible about Balaam, I had a complete understanding of what was happening. I see how God will find a way to communicate with you to get your attention. As I read, I got a surge of revelation about my past and current situations, and I was comforted by God's willingness to direct me. So many memories and aha moments rushed into my mind. It felt like information overload. It was as if my mind was being flooded with knowledge and understanding.

I stopped reading and took a deep breath. I had a strange sense of peace in this surreal moment. I felt comforted, like my help had finally come. I looked over at Lavender while she was licking her paw.

"Lavender, I still can't get over the fact that you're talking to me."Well, get used to it. My mouth has been opened to communicate with you so I can help you know the Holy Spirit. It's the Holy Spirit that enables you to follow God. If you don't have the Holy Spirit, how can you obey Him? Remember what you read in the Book of John? John 14:17-18 states, 'The world is unable to receive Him because it doesn't see Him or know Him. But you do know Him, because He remains with you and will be in you. I will not leave you as orphans; I am coming to you.' You prayed for the Holy Spirit and you have received it! God opened my mouth so I can help you know the Holy Spirit. Just like when Balaam's donkey talked, the purpose was to help Balaam see the path he was going would lead to destruction. Nicole,

God wants you on the right path. Emptiness is not something a child of God should possess. If you belong to the Life Giver and He put His Spirit in you, then life will be your portion forever. You're thirty years old now. Don't keep living how you were—hopeless and desolate. I was sent to guide you because, just like Balaam, you don't take hints very well. Today, your life is different; you now possess the Holy Spirit. It is the Spirit of God. He is the Truth, Helper, and Comforter. It is His Spirit that draws you near to God. Without His Spirit, you cannot obey God."

I paused. "Whoa, I didn't know any of that. Wait, let me get this straight—I was being hard-headed like this man Balaam, and God opened your mouth to enable you to communicate with me?"

"Yes, and it's because you need to learn. Hosea spoke correctly when he said, 'My people are destroyed for lack of knowledge.' Nicole, you need to learn. Everyday, I am going to help you read the Bible. I want you to think about the verses, and if you don't understand something, pray for wisdom about it. This is to help you grow. God wants His people to know Him, and how can you know Him apart from His Word?"

Lavender put her paw on the Bible and said, "This is His Word. Get familiar with it. Learn it and watch how the Word will change your life."

Journal Entry 1/4/2019

My life has changed so dramatically. As I am writing this down, everything seems like a movie. It doesn't feel like real life anymore. Aside from my cat communicating with me daily, everything is the same, except my demeanor. I feel happy and joyful. I enjoy reading the Bible and praying. Sometimes, I feel so close to God—it's as if He is talking to me as I read the Bible. It's almost a tangible feeling. The peace that seems to flow out of me is constant. My life has improved. Even people at work have noticed that I seem to be glowing. Another big deal is that I am more loving to people, and it's a genuine love. I am no longer a fake lover of people, but a sincere lover of people. I even forgave all my exes. This was something I didn't even know I still had issues with. Another huge change is that I started praying for my boss, Diva. I no longer hate her. In fact, I feel sorry for her because she doesn't seem to have this joy that I have. Nowadays, I talk about helping people and what I can do to help. I can't even believe I want to go out of my way for others now. This feeling is exciting!

Journal Entry 2/10/2019

I don't even know where to begin. Life is awesome! January was a month of miracles for me. I changed so much because the Holy Spirit that is in me is helping me. Lavender is a good teacher; if I have a question, she will tell me to turn to a book in the Bible and look for the answer in a passage of scripture. Work is now enjoyable; I am getting along with everyone. I want to tell everybody about becoming a real Christian! I want to ask people who do profess to be Christians, "Do you have the Holy

Spirit?" If not, you have got to get Him!" Lately, Lavender has been busy with telling me to read more in depth—to not be so focused on the blessing, but to read about how God will allow you to face trials. She told me to read through the book of Judges and to think about how the people of Israel felt when they were being oppressed. Yesterday, she even brought me a notebook to take notes about the questions or revelations I get while reading through the book of Judges. When I asked her why she was being so extra with the homework, she simply said, "I just want you to be prepared." I wonder what she meant by that. Aren't I already prepared? After all, I have the Holy Spirit. If God is on my side, who can be against me? If at the name of Jesus every knee shall bow and every tongue confess that Jesus Christ is Lord, what do I need to be afraid of? Every situation, person, place or thing is subject to Christ, so what do I need to be prepared for?

Lavender hadn't spoken in three weeks; she'd reverted back to a normal cat. I missed our conversations and Bible studies. She'd started back to meowing in the morning so I could let her go outside. For a few days, Lavender's morning routine consisted of waking me up with excessive meowing and lingering in the bathroom while I brushed my teeth and washed my face. After this, she would run to the kitchen to get a nibble of some of her food. Once I got my tea, I would venture out onto the patio with Lavender following closely behind me. I would normally sip on my tea and read my Bible out on the patio. Lavender was always nearby, lounging in a sunspot by the potted plants.

It was just a typical morning. I didn't feel like sitting out on the patio that day, so I was going to let Lavender out by herself. I was going to sit at the kitchen table to drink my tea and read. I walked over to the patio door to let out Lavender, and that's when I felt the room change.

The temperature didn't change, but I felt uneasy and the air in the room became stagnant. The air seemed thick and it became harder for me to breathe. I felt light-headed and nauseous. As I put my hand on the doorknob to open it so I could get some fresh air, I heard loud footsteps coming from the patio door. It sounded as if someone was running down a hallway. The footsteps were getting louder and louder. Frightened by the sound of the footsteps near the back door, I jolted away from the door, grabbed Lavender and turned to run. Before I could dart and hide, I heard the locked door slowly creak open. My back was turned towards the door and I was scared motionless. My heart dropped and I completely froze. All I could hear was my heart beating. A shadow entered through the crack underneath the door. Lavender hissed and growled as the shadow seeped through the crack. The shadow poured onto the floor like a liquid. I finally mustered up the courage to turn around and I saw the shadow in a puddle on the floor. I wanted to run out of the house, but I was too scared to move. I tried to inch away from the door, but the shadow stretched closer to me and grew in size. After that, I started to panic and looked around to figure out how I could get away. As it inched closer to me, I screamed: "Jesus, help me!" Immediately after I screamed out the name Jesus, the shadow violently jerked back to the door and manifested into a shape of a person. The evil spirit spoke. "Hey, take it easy. I wasn't trying to scare you. I just wanted to tell you that I have a great opportunity for you. I happened to be roaming to-and-fro when I noticed that you seemed a bit distracted." Lavender jumped out of my arms and growled at the evil spirit. The evil spirit said,"Nicole, you know what's up? This journey you're trying to entertain won't get you far. You don't need to say His name or anything. I come in peace. Look, I can give you what you want. I have been aware of you since you were a little girl. You don't need this Holy Spirit. I can give you everything and more."

The living room walls began to fade and then, fall just like a curtain. Suddenly, I was in front of a huge mansion. I could hear people arguing inside. The evil spirit walked up the stairs and opened the door. A woman pulling luggage stormed out of the house. "I hate you! You never loved me! All you ever did was compare me to your exes!" I watched her with my eyes.

"She looks very familiar," I thought to myself. The evil spirit appeared near my side.

"She was your best friend in high school. How could you forget that she stole your boyfriend and had the audacity to marry him too? Remember how much you hated her for that? Well, now it's your chance to steal something from her. Look at this mansion. Isn't it huge? Come on, Nicole. You live in a shack compared to this place. Did you see the car she drove off in? Such grandeur and fine living. She is living the life you should be living; don't you agree?"

I couldn't even think. I just stared. Memories came flooding back into my mind. I remember how crushed I felt five years ago when I'd heard they'd gotten married.

The evil spirit spoke again. "I don't want to rub it in, but it looks like you lost. This is what happens when you are the good girl. People take advantage of you. Don't you want all of this? I'll give it to you. All I need is your agreement. Just agree with my plan and listen to me. See a couple of my comrades have been watching this family for me. This couple is on the brink of divorce. We worked hard all year for it to come to this. Now that she has left her husband, the cat's already in the bag! Now, this is where you come in. I need you to contact him; that's it. I will make him worship the ground you walk on, and in six months, he will be your husband. See how simple it is?! It's so easy, Nicole! We have done all the background work. All you need to do is come in and seal the deal. Now, there is a minor issue that will present itself later down the road. In about three years, you must divorce him because I really need this guy to suffer. He kicked out my buddy from this mansion a couple of months ago, and boy is he back with a vengeance, along with seven others more vicious than him! Look, I know it's a lot to take in, but trust me."

He stretched out his hand to shake mine. "Do we have a deal?"

While the evil spirit was talking, I did feel angry towards the couple. Memories brought back the painful heartbreak I'd experienced because of them. To be honest, a part of me wanted to get even. However, there was a strong resistance in my spirit. I just couldn't hurt someone like that. I didn't want to cause heartbreak to someone else. I know what that feels like, and I didn't want to do that to them. I didn't want them to experience heartbreak because of me. At that moment, the love in me overtook the hate in me.

"I can't," I said.

"Hey now! Don't be so hasty. Maybe you don't realize how easy your job would be."

Suddenly, I was in a huge room. It looked like a couture showroom. There was even a crystal chandelier hanging from the ceiling. Everything was high-end and luxurious. The clothes were neatly organized by season and color. There was an entire wall dedicated to purses and handbags. Everything was displayed so beautifully. There was even a shoe room. "This place is wonderful," I thought to myself. I walked over to a couple of the pieces to touch them and noticed that it was all my size.

The evil spirit appeared again. "This is your closet. Everything in here is yours."
The evil spirit sat down on a chair by the mirror. "Let me tell you how easy your life would be. Number one, you won't have to work at all. Number two, you will be rich. Number three, I will give you whatever you want. You just need to be my vessel. Let me use you on the earth to accomplish some things."
He got up from the chair and walked towards me. He extended his hand for me to shake.

"Do we have a deal?"

I stepped away from its hand. I knew that if I shook that demon's hand, I would be completely out of the will of God. I learned that I can only serve one master. If I shake its hand, then I reject God. How could I reject my Lord? He died for me. He fights for me. He is my only help. He is my rest. Scripture after scripture began to flow into my mind about the goodness of God and how there is no other way but Him. "Nicole, I've been watching you and I know your desires. I just want to help you fulfill those desires. I can guide you. Let me teach you the right way to live. You think being a Christian will help you? It's a lie. Here take my hand and I will help you."
It extended its hand towards me once more. I stood there suddenly feeling fearless. At that moment, I understood what was going on. The enemy was asking me if I would serve him—if I would commit my life to him. The Bible tells stories upon stories about how people were

tested and what choices they'd made. In the time of testing, who you really are comes out. I vaguely remembered in the book of Matthew, how Jesus was tested in the wilderness. I used to think tests would be easy to pass, but that experience was leaving me hesitant. All that I wanted was within hand's reach. Am I a bad person for looking? I looked at the riches and contemplated in my heart the things this evil spirit offered me. I knew it was wrong, but there was something inside me that was interested in what that devil had to offer.

I remembered when the believers of great faith were faced with trials, they ultimately followed God and trusted Him. From Genesis to Revelation, I am commanded to follow God and trust only Him. I wondered if I was experiencing the same feelings Esther had experienced when she faced going to the king without being summoned. Did she ever think, "I could continue living comfortably if I ignore the issue?" Did she ever regret her decision after it passed her lips? However, she made the choice to obey God. When she uttered, "If I perish, I perish," she'd made the decision to follow God. The God I serve is worth the total commitment. Esther knew that it's not worth it to live independently of God; she knew that in the face of temptation to turn towards God. I stood amid all my wants and desires and turned my back on them to serve God. I made up my mind that He is worth the commitment. In the face of temptation, I turned to my Lord and Savior and pledged my allegiance to Him alone. Even though the devil offered me something I legitimately wanted, I could not accept bribes from the enemy. I couldn't become a vessel used for wickedness. Once I made up my mind, I felt as though my faith in Jesus Christ became a tangible thing. I felt strength come over me. I felt enraged that a demon had invaded my house and offered me complete and utter destruction. I looked at the evil spirit's shadowy hand. Boldness consumed me and I got angry at it. Without me realizing it, I smacked its shadowy hand away from me and yelled. "No, I will serve God! Get away from me!"

The evil spirit was relentless. "Don't make me angry. I am trying to be nice. Take the offer or else!"

I stood my ground and looked right into its wicked eyes.

"Go away! I'm not serving you!" I yelled with even more power in my voice.

Wicked laughter echoed throughout the room. "You stupid human. Don't you know what we do to people who decline our offers?"

Chapter 5

SAVED

Thick darkness surrounded me and I could not see. I thought I had died because, in that moment, I was at peace. I knew in my heart that I'd committed my life to God and that He would take care of me. Is this how the three Hebrew boys felt when they were walking around in the furnace unbound and unharmed? Did the same peace overtake them that overtook me? I recalled a thought that ran through my mind while I stood in silence. "I am alone, yet I am not alone. I am in total darkness, yet consumed with eternal light."

I didn't know where I was, but I knew that God was with me. What is in me won't abandon me. This situation reminded me of Psalm 139:7-10. It reads, "Where shall I go from your Spirit? Or where shall I flee from your presence? If I ascend to heaven, you are there! If I make my bed in Sheol, you are there! If I take the wings of the morning and dwell in the uttermost parts of the sea, even there your hand shall lead me, and your right hand shall hold me."

When the Psalm verse came to mind, my spirit became stirred and I prayed quietly. "Lord, thank you for being with me. You put your Spirit in me and I am your child. The one whom you love, the apple of your eye. Thank you for never leaving me or forsaking me." As I prayed to myself, I looked at my hand and I could see light beaming out of the lines in my hands. A soft voice spoke amid the darkness. It said, "The Spirit of God, who raised Jesus from the dead, lives in you. And just as God raised Christ Jesus from the dead, he will give life to your mortal bodies by this same Spirit living within you" (Romans 8:11).

In the blink of an eye, I was suddenly back in my bed and my Bible was on my lap; it was opened to the Book of Romans with chapter eight, verse eleven highlighted in yellow. I couldn't say anything. I sat on my bed and prayed to God. I praised Him for being my Protector and Savior. I don't know what happened or how to explain what had transpired; all I know is that I am never alone.

The next day, I got up to go to work. I looked over at the patio door and thought to myself, "Was all that a dream?" Surprisingly, I wasn't afraid, however, I was confused. The only conclusion I could come to was I must have been dreaming. Once I got to work, I still could not focus. I kept thinking about the demonic encounter. Was it all a dream? Was I really tempted by a devil in real life? Why was I in that dark place? What about the light that was in my hands; what was that? My mind kept replaying what happened; it was like a movie reel. I never knew stuff like that could happen. Lavender being able to talk seemed like child's play compared to that scary experience. I remember before Lavender stopped talking, she told me to read through the book of Judges. I still didn't understand how the Book of Judges had anything to do with what I went through, but I felt like Lavender had left a clue for me to investigate. I thought about what stuck out to me when I read through the Book of Judges. I remembered people fighting the Philistines and the strong guy Samson, but I couldn't think of a situation in Judges where a demon had tempted someone.

After work, I rushed home. I opened the door to find Lavender sleeping on the couch. I yelled at her, "Can you talk yet?!" She jumped up from her slumber with a startled meow. Disappointed by her response, I headed to my room to get my Bible. Judges 2:1-3 stuck out to me. "The angel of the Lord went up from Gilgal to Bokim and said, 'I brought you up out of Egypt and led you into the land I swore to give to your ancestors.' I said, 'I will never break my covenant with you, and you shall not make a covenant with the people of this land, but you shall break down their altars.' Yet you have disobeyed me. Why have you done this? And I have also said, 'I will not drive them out before you; they will become traps for you, and their gods will become snares to you.'"

 I read over the three verses another time. What stuck out to me was the word snares— "and their gods will become snares to you." So, is God saying if idols are not removed, they will eventually trap you? I couldn't help but dwell on the third verse. I got my journal and started writing my thoughts.

Journal Entry 3/15/2019

What am I holding inside of me that is a snare to me? Is it unforgiveness or materialism? Could these things be used by the devil as a trap? Is it because I still haven't forgiven? Did unforgiveness allow the enemy to come into my life and entice me? What would have happened if I had not been getting closer to God and growing into a mature Christian? Would I have accepted the devil's bait?

The more I thought about it, the more I became even more concerned about the state of my heart. I had to admit that, at one point, I did want to accept the evil spirit's offer, but I felt like love rose up from within me and changed my mind.

I sighed deeply and thought to myself, "All this thinking is making me tired." I didn't know where to go for help and I was too afraid to ask people about what my experience meant because I didn't want people to think I'd lost my mind. "Lord, please help me," I prayed. "This has me feeling overwhelmed."

I woke up late since I didn't have to go to work the next day. I was in the process of getting up to do my usual routine of drinking tea and reading. I got up, stretched and turned to look at Lavender sleeping on the edge of my bed. "Good morning, Vendy," I said while yawning. Lavender looked at me and replied with a soft, "Good morning."

"Ahh! You scared me!" I screamed. "You should warn me before you start talking out of the blue like that," I said to her.

"I suppose I could warn you first."

"Oh my goodness I have so much to talk to you about!"

"You do know that I am going to refer you to a bunch of Bible verses. Get your Bible and note-book."

"I'm too confused to read my Bible. Can't you just tell me what in the world is happening in my life? You know my life got weird when you started talking. Now, I'm getting harassed by evil spirits! I thought if I received the Holy Spirit, life would be easy. I'm still working at my lame job, I have no deep relationships with people—what's the point? Where is the Comforter? I'm not being comforted right now or helped; I am on my own just like I was before I started praying. The only thing I received from praying for the Holy Spirit is a headache."

Lavender placed her paw on my leg as I sat up on my bed. She looked intently at me with her bright greenish-yellow eyes.

"Nicole, you need to decide now! I came here to help you, but if you think this Christian life is a walk in the park with zero issues, then I will stop talking. What do you think the Bible is about? Everyone in the Bible had a choice to make. Am I going to serve the only True God? You are sad because a demon provoked you? You're a Christian—you are going to be pro-voked! The devil hates you just because you serve Jesus Christ. Of course, you will be at-tacked, but don't you realize how you have overcome? Do you remember the three He-brew boys that Nebuchadnezzar had thrown into the fiery furnace? They weren't thrown in the fire for no reason; they were hated because they served the only True God. The devil uses human beings to persecute the children of God. Jesus said it out of His own mouth. John 16:33 (NIV) states, 'In this world you will have trouble. But take heart! I have overcome the world.' Jesus told us that He has overcome the world. If He put His Overcoming Spirit in you, then you will overcome the world too. If God saved those men thrown in the fiery furnace, then He will save you too."

Lavender then jumped off the bed and I watched her go into the kitchen to eat her cat food.

I wasn't expecting to hear Lavender say what she'd said. She didn't feel sorry for me at all. She'd told me point blank that it's not a game—I had to make up my mind who I would serve.

I had to leave the house to clear my mind. I wasn't expecting to get reprimanded by my pet cat, but she was right. After the weighty lecture I got from Lavender, I wanted to get some fresh air and walk around to recollect my thoughts. I drove to a nearby high school and parked by the track. I tried to jog a little, but I ended up walking slowly in lane eight. Since no one was around, I started to talk out loud to myself. Lavender was right, I need to stop whining and just be a Christian. When she was talking to me, I felt convicted. How could I forget that God was with me during the attack? When I was in a pit of darkness, I was comforted and protected. I didn't know where I was, but I was rescued. I was taken out of thick darkness and placed on my bed.

I continued to walk laps on the track and dwelt on when God was with me during times of hardship and how He'd rescued me from situations. I wanted to continue growing and maturing as a Christian. I vowed not to become discouraged; I vowed to continue in the faith. I will set my face as flint and live the life God has for me.

The wind began to pick up and I could tell Spring was here. I stopped to look towards the field that was next to the track. Bluebonnets spread out on the ground like a blanket. I could see families taking pictures in the distance with the popular state flower. Everyone looked so excited to take pictures in their matching out-fits. I smiled to myself and breathed in the fresh air of Spring. I noticed more of the beauty of nature as I walked around the track. The bright dandelions were busting out the cracks of the concrete sidewalk. The freshly manicured grass in the middle of the track was lush and green. I could even hear the mockingbirds chirping nearby and a red cardinal was singing while sitting on a tree branch. My mood com-pletely changed in that moment. Instead of feeling agitated and convicted, I was joyful.

Spring was in full bloom in Dallas and the showroom of Stacie Pearl had fully embraced it. The color of the season was green, and ev-erything was green. The customers loved it and women were coming in droves to buy the new Spring collections.

While I was dressing one of the mannequins in a pastel green silk wrap dress, Natalie handed me a green silk scarf. She said, "Diva wants more green on the mannequin."

"Really? Okay. I get that green is in this season, but it looks a lot like St. Patrick's Day in here."

"Why not tie the scarf around her head like a pirate? Let's start a new trend."

"Leprechaun meets pirate. I love it!"

Natalie and I laughed amongst ourselves while she helped me dress more mannequins.

At that time, I had been feeling overwhelmed with people and a break from work was much-needed for me. I wanted to have some alone time to reflect. I managed to get a month off by using up all my paid time off. Lavender had been talking again. She'd encouraged me to take a break and just hang out with God. I liked how she phrased it—"Just hang out with God."

The next day, I had planned to tell the Diva that I was taking a month-long vacation. I'd planned to tell her before she left for the day. At exactly two that afternoon, I made a beeline to her office near the stock room. The conversation I had with her was surprisingly calm. The whole chat confirmed that God wanted me to take a break. I told Diva I was going to be using up all my vacation time to take the month of April off and she said, "Sure." What really shocked me was what she said afterward. "Nicole, I really appreciate all that you've done as co-manager so enjoy your vacation, and I look forward to seeing you in May." There was no attitude—she didn't even look me up and down. She was surprisingly nice. "Wow", I said to myself, "Thank you, Lord. That was incredibly easy." I thought I was going to have to darn near quit to get that month off. So, this is what it feels like to have angels go before you to protect you along the way and to bring you to the place God has prepared (Exodus 23:20). I'd read that in my Bible the day prior.

After I returned from my vacation, I started using work as an opportunity to pray for people. Some of the customers were open and told me about their lives. I would always leave them with, "I will pray for you." The first couple of times I did this, I'd startled a few people, but overall, people like prayer. I noticed that as soon as I said, "I will pray for you," their disposition would always get better.

One day, I was busy dressing the mannequins and steaming clothes, so I wasn't having much interaction with customers. While I was in the stockroom getting new clothes for the mannequins, I heard my coworker Juana walk in. "Nicole, you back here?"

"Yep, I'm back here steaming clothes; what's up?"

Juana sarcastically replied, "The return king is here and is requesting you."

"Oh, my favorite customer is here. Okay. I'll take care of it."

Now Herman, the return king, was a retired investment banker who had been sent by his
wife to return clothes she'd bought from the
store. Once a week, he would come in to return
and chat. He would tell me about his adventures as an investment banker in New Orleans.
My favorite story of his was when he went on a
swamp boat tour and lost his glasses during
the boat's takeoff and couldn't see a thing. He
said the only thing he got from the trip was a
sunburn on the top of his head. He was fun to
talk to. I personally believed he used those re-
turns to get out of the house.

"My favorite manager! How are you?!"
"Hey Hermon, how are you? I didn't see you
last week. Did you go out of town?
"I have been sick lately."
"I can't have my favorite customer getting sick.
I will pray for your healing!"
"Oh okay. Well—uh—thanks."

Chapter 6

IN THE SPRING TIME

There had been more rain in April than usual. Spring time in Texas is nice; the temperature isn't too hot and there is always a cool breeze. This is the time the wildflowers begin to bloom and paint the fields in an assortment of colors. I remembered the reason I'd fallen in love with my condo. It was because it had a nice patio deck with a covering. From there, I could sit underneath and look out at the park across from me. Whenever I sat outside, the fresh scent of the soil and trees would rise from the park. Lavender loved the patio as well; she would lounge by the potted plants or sit next to me on the patio bench. We both enjoyed nature. It makes me feel calm and helps me to clear my mind.

Lately, I had been excited about morning devotions. Ever since I took the month off, I made it a point to have a dedicated time for morning devotions. I wake up around seven in the morning, read the Bible and pray until eight. The first week had been very relaxing. In fact, the atmosphere was very peaceful. Once I stepped inside my house from running errands, I was completely at peace—no matter what was on my mind. At home, I felt cool, calm and collected. I really enjoyed the feeling.

It was a Sunday morning when I sat down at my kitchen table to open my Bible. I was reading through the Book of Samuel, and as I read "In the Spring when kings march out to war," I could smell fresh rain and the room became quiet. I waited at the kitchen table, expectant for something significant to happen. I stopped reading and looked around. I leaned over to check to see if I'd left the patio door open because the scent of the room was different. I could smell rain and wild flowers. As I breathed in the fresh aroma, I noticed that the large clock on the wall wasn't ticking and even the steam from my tea had stopped moving. Suddenly, I could no longer speak. My ability to speak was gone, but I knew I was speaking through my thoughts. I had a sense of knowing and a feeling of familiarity, as if this was normal.

A door of pure light formed before my eyes. An angel clothed in light that flowed like liquid entered through the door. He nodded to me then walked to the coffee table and pulled out a chair. He stood next to it.

I was overwhelmed, yet calm. My eyes were fixed on the man who'd entered through the light. He wore royal garments and the colors were so rich that I couldn't describe them. He was tall in stature with a ruddy complexion. I had a sense of knowing that the man was King David. He sat down in the chair across from me. He looked at me intently and spoke. His words had vision and impact—so much so that I could visibly see and feel each sentence. I felt like I had experienced what he'd spoken.

King David said to me, "I was given the ability

to come visit and to share with you what I'd learned on Earth. This is so you, in turn, can live how God wants you to live. I know you are a child of God; we are family. If you didn't belong to the Kingdom of God, I would not be sitting before you. As a brother in Christ, I will share with you what I learned on Earth. Too much thinking will frustrate you, so keep it simple. Keep your mind on fulfilling the will of God. This will save you from many sorrows and pain. While I was on the Earth, I would often think about the creeping enemy or the approaching darkness. When King Saul sought to kill me, I would often become discouraged and feel vulnerable. Fear almost consumed me when I thought about the impending ambush from my adversaries. Yet, what kept me from falling into the pit of despair was the mercy of God. When I was poured out like water and my heart melted within me, I cried out to the Lord and He rescued me. He hears the cries of His children, and those cries stir His compassionate heart. Just like a mother, He won't forget the child He's birthed. It was not my deeds that saved me or my skill with the sword. I was not able to save myself; my army was not strong enough, my horses were not swift enough, and my sword was not sharp enough. Only God could pull me out of the blazing fire. Only God was with me when I made my bed in death. I recall looking at my hands stained with the blood of men. I said to myself, 'What am I that God would care to think of me? Aren't we all made from the dirt? Aren't we all nothing?' Yet, because of His great mercy, we live forever. I was a man abandoned and rejected, but I was shown mercy. What saved me was the pure mercy of God. By His command, I was kept alive to complete my assignments on Earth. May this be your testimony on Earth. 'Great is your mercy towards me, goodness and mercy shall follow me all the days of my life. And at the end of my life the word of God was in my mouth.'"

As he spoke, I felt like my insides were about

to burst with joy. I could feel how he felt, and my spirit was stirred inside of me.

King David got up from his seat. The angel escorted him to the door of light, and before they walked through the door, David turned to me and said. "I will see you again when you make it home." They walked through the door of light and disappeared. The room changed and time started again. The steam from my tea slowly rose, and then dissipated into the air. I sat quietly in my kitchen and considered all the words King David had just spoken to me. I was so overtaken with joy that I started crying. I was crying when 1Corinthians 2:9-10 popped into my head. It reads, "What no eye has seen what no ear has heard, and what no human mind has conceived the things God has prepared for those who love him these are the things God has revealed to us by his Spirit."

I knew that was the Holy Spirit bringing this verse to my remembrance. I was so grateful that God was so loving that He'd decided to let me meet someone from the Bible. I felt just like King David when he said, "Who am I that you are mindful of me?" I never would have imagined that I would have a heavenly encounter. I was content with reading the Bible. I had never imagined that it would be possible to experience signs, miracles and wonders. In that moment, I realized that having the Holy Spirit is definitely a life-changer. The Bible was no longer just a book to me. Through the Holy Spirit, it comes alive and the people I read about become real. I've learned about how God saves and how He pours out mercy and goodness on his children. On that memorable day, I tasted and seen that the Lord is good.

Lavender walked over to my chair and pawed at my leg to get my attention. She said, "So, what did you learn from your experience?"
"Did you see it too?"
"Yeah, I was watching while I catnapped by the window."

"Well, I learned that God is merciful and He will come to the aid of His children. It made me want to continue to serve God. I want to be like King David and be able to say to my brothers and sisters in Christ, 'See you again when you make it home.' I want to be able to encourage someone to keep on living for God. I want to help others make it home."

"Write it down so you can remember the gift God gave you today. Thank the Lord for giving you revelation about His mercy. Thank the Lord for giving you a key to help you live for God on Earth. Thank Him for His Spirit that He put in you."

I grabbed my journal from my nightstand and wrote. For the rest of the day, I was in bliss. I felt euphoric—like I was floating the whole day. I was excited about knowing God and getting closer to Him.

Chapter 7

REST

It was a Thursday and I'd woken up bursting with energy. I made a to-do list to clean up the house. I'd planned on going to meet up with friends for lunch. After that, I would end the day with a jog at the high school track near me. Lavender looked at me as I was rushing around the house. She walked over to me and started speaking. "Why are you so busy right now? You didn't open your Bible to read this morning."

"I will read it later; I need to run to the store to buy paper towels."

"At least eat something for breakfast. It's not good to rush into your day. The best thing I can teach you is to enter your day with communication with God. Make it normal to wake up and pray. Before you do anything in the morning, talk with God."

What Lavender said was true. I had woken up without acknowledging God at all. Even though the plans I'd made for the day seem insignificant, I still needed to include my Heavenly Father into my daily schedule. When I was a little girl living in my parents' house, I had to tell my dad if I wanted to walk to the store to get a snack or go outside to play with a friend. Those things seemed small, but I still had to tell my dad what I was doing. All the same, I am a child of God, so I must include Him in my daily affairs and ask Him what He thinks about my plans.

I sat down at the kitchen table to eat the breakfast I'd prepared. I picked up some scrambled eggs with my fork, and before the food could reach my mouth, I was suddenly zapped into a dense, yet colorful jungle. I still had on my pajamas, but I was barefoot. I looked around and this place was unlike anything I had ever seen before. The trees were marvelous and the sound of the leaves rustling in the wind sounded like quiet chimes. All the shades of green were radiant and bright. The fruits were large and the sweet aroma of them filled the atmosphere. Everything was magnificent, even the birds were chirping sounds I'd never heard before. Peace and serenity were all I felt. I didn't know where I was, but I wanted to stay there. I noticed there was no shade or shadows. If a tree towered over a plant, there was no shadow of the tree —only the light of the tree. It was a magnificent sight to behold. As I looked around and marveled at the scenery, I was startled by a thunderous voice, "Let us make man in our image." I didn't know where it had come from, so I looked towards the East.

I stood behind a tree and peeked to see what was happening. I watched as a human was forged out of the womb of the earth. The body lay lifeless on the ground until the breath of God entered him and he breathed his first breath. He rose up and walked with God towards a garden. I wanted to follow them. I wanted to walk with God. I felt like a child following her father. As I chased after Him, I found myself back in my kitchen. Everything was back to normal but me. I wanted what

Adam had. I thought to myself, "How can I walk with God? I want that relationship. I want that closeness." I opened my Bible and turned to the Book of Genesis.

I read about the story of creation and how God made man. Then an angel stood in front of the kitchen table I was sitting at. He talked to me without alerting me to the fact that I had another house guest. He escorted a man in through a door of light. I knew who he was before he sat down. Adam was in my kitchen.

"I am Adam," he boldly said.
"When I was born, I was a borrowed breath from the Creator. I lived because He gave me life. I breathed because He put the breath of life in me. How are you any different from me? I walked with God in the cool of the Garden, but you walk with Him as well. I was made and put in God's rest—the Garden of Eden—a special place. The place of rest is where God always intended us to be. Heaven on Earth has always

been our portion. Listen to what I have to say. Walk with God always and never hide. Take a walk with Life and live. That is our purpose to walk and talk with the Creator. My Father birthed me from the ground. I came from nothing. I was mere clay, but God put His Spirit in dirt, and I lived. Weren't you nothing before He breathed life into you? You were dead too before He put His Spirit in you. The close relationship you desired when you saw me and the Father walking together, you already have it. What more is there in life than to walk with the Almighty God in the cool of the Garden? My Life, my Lord, and my God was walking next to me. Listen to the words of the first man of the Earth. Walk with God. He is loving and willing to walk with the lesser. For we are all dirt with the Holy One's breath in us, allowing us to live and exist. I am clay that was formed by the Master. I am Adam, the one formed by the hands of God."

Adam was escorted to the door of light, and with a flash, he was gone. This encounter was different. I was in Eden and saw the beauty with my own eyes. It left me with a longing to go back. Ever since then, I have not felt so attached to the things of this world anymore because I desired to be like Adam. I wanted to walk with God. I repeated in my head what he'd said about how I walk with God as well. Maybe Adam was saying that I am already walking with God because I have the Holy Spirit. I sat at the kitchen table, took a bite of my food and thought about all of what I had seen and heard.

Lavender looked over at me as she ate her food.

"How do you feel after being in the Garden of Eden and talking with Adam?"

"It made me homesick. I felt like that place was home. What did Adam mean when he said I already walk with God?"

Lavender finished lapping up her water before she answered me.

"Read Galatians chapter five, starting at verse 13. Read all the way to the end of the chapter.

It talks about living by the Spirit, and I think that will give you some insight on how to walk with God.

Chapter 8

I CAN SEE

I woke up early the next day. It was five o'clock in the morning and it was still dark outside. I tried to go back to sleep, but I felt led to get up and read my Bible. I made a cup of chamomile tea to help me go back to sleep, and after the tea was ready, I sat at my kitchen table to read. I opened the Bible without a book or chapter in mind. It fell opened to the Book of Judges, chapter 13—the story of Samson.

A doorway of light appeared in front of me. An angel escorted a man into my kitchen. Everything became still and I couldn't speak. Peace consumed the atmosphere. I fixed my gaze on the man sitting across from me. He was familiar; it was as if I was meeting a friend I hadn't seen in a while. He had on radiant garments that were so bright, they glowed. Additionally, his hair was platted in seven long beautiful braids. He looked at me before speaking. Samson said to me, "I am Samson, God's strong man. I was escorted here from Heaven to share with you some advice. God thought my words would help you, so listen up! Change your appetite! Nicole, what is it that your flesh craves? Is it money, power, or do you lust after relationships? When I was living on Earth, I did not live up to the standard that God had for me. I was a Nazarite, dedicated to God in the womb. Yet, when I grew up, I had an appetite for things that did not please God. Once I ate honey from a dead lion, which was an unclean thing. Now, that doesn't seem too bad, right? But if you look at it through discerning eyes, It means I sought sweet things from unclean sources. I wanted the good things in life, but I got them from the wrong sources. Honey is a good thing, but getting it from a carcass isn't the right way to get it. I even had an appetite for women who did not believe in my God. In fact, they served idols. Little did I know, I would end up bound in a temple of one of their idols. My lifestyle did not match who I was. I was a servant of the Most High God, but I wasn't living in accordance with His standards. Because

I was spiritually blind by not seeing what God was doing in my life, I was physically blinded by my enemies. Because I was weak in my relationship with God by not living in accordance with His will, I became physically weak when God took His strength from me. Because I was spiritually bound by my lustful appetite which, of course, is idolatry, I became physically bound in the temple of an idol. Learn from how I lived my life on Earth. Gratifying the desires of your flesh will never end well. I enjoyed whatever, whenever and it left me as a chained fool in the face of my enemies. My wild lifestyle left me bound and blinded in a pagan temple. However, God is truly merciful. Did you know when you surrender to God, He will have mercy on you? When my eyes were gouged out by the enemy and I was tied with bronze shackles, I was imprisoned and forced to grind grain. But God remembered me. With my arms stretched out to the temple pillars, I looked up to heaven and surrendered. God heard my prayer. He gave me one more opportunity to be used by

Him. When I cried out to God, He showed me mercy and renewed my strength. He gave me one last chance to get it right. I killed more at the point of my death than I'd done when I was alive. In my weakness, I poured out my life and He made me strong once again. It's true that when you are weak, the Lord will make you strong."

Without any notice, there was a flash of light, and in the blink of an eye, Samson was gone. I sat at the table and looked down at my cup of tea. It was still steaming hot. Meeting with Samson was convicting. His speech was short, but intense. He spoke very sternly to me like he was trying to keep me from making the same mistakes he'd made.

Lavender interrupted my thoughts. She said, "So, what did you learn from Samson?"
"You saw that? I thought you were sleeping."
"I got up when you did, and I've been here the whole time."

"Well, I learned a lot from that encounter. What he said was convicting. How I live does matter. I used to think there was no wrong way to live, but according to Samson, there is. Now I understand why Moses cried out to the people of Israel. Deuteronomy 30:19-20 (NIV) reads, 'I have set before you life and death, blessings and curses. Now choose life, so that you and your children may live and that you may love the Lord your God, listen to his voice, and hold fast to him. For the Lord is your life.' There are consequences for my decisions. Samson warned me not to live for myself, and I decided to take his advice. I realized that there is a price associated with my choices, and what I harbor inside of me can give me victory or defeat."

Still thinking about my conversation with Samson, I finished my cup of tea and dragged myself to bed. As I drifted off to sleep, I felt the wind sweep across my face. I assumed it was the air conditioner turning on. I rolled over, but I

was no longer in my bed. I was standing outside near a desert.

Hot wind blew against my face. I shut my eyes
and covered my face with a linen scarf. The
wind was blowing so strong that the sand was
being picked up and it was whirling around me.
I turned and peered through the sandy blizzard
and saw a beautiful city. Unexpectedly,
someone pulled my arm and said, "Come
quickly! Don't look back." I was in the middle of
a caravan. Herds of sheep walked by me and
two shepherd boys darted past me as they
played with one another. The children had no
idea what was happening.

The atmosphere was heavy from the weight of
a serious decision. The wind died down and I
could see more of the people traveling. I
glanced over to the left and saw Abraham. He
was a tall man wearing fine linen. His
expression was solemn. I knew exactly what
he was feeling without him saying anything. He

had left all that he knew to follow God—a God
he had never seen, only heard. He is the father
of faith; he trusted God without seeing Him. He
moved without a discussion. I was part of the
caravan leaving Haran. In my heart, I
understood Abraham's emotions. I am sure
others have asked, "Why give up all that you
know to follow God?" I saw Abraham turn to
me. When he looked me in my eyes, the desert
began to fade away and I found myself sitting
at my kitchen table. Abraham was sitting
across from me. The father of the faith opened
his mouth to speak to me.

"I am Abraham, the man who decided to trust
God. The love of God will make you give it all
up for Him. I left Haran and the life I knew
because God called me forth. I couldn't help
but obey the command of the lover of my soul.
For He summoned me out of darkness and
brought me into light. He guided me out of my
father's house and brought me to my
inheritance. He will be a good shepherd to you,
just as He was to me. I was never abandoned

nor forsaken. He was merciful to me, even when I sinned. He poured out love and kindness on me all the days of my life. I gave up what I knew and gained what I'd never known. He gave me an inheritance that I never could have imaged. If you find the act of obedience hard, simply take one foot at a time. Just put one foot in front of the other. You don't need all the information upfront; just obey the little information you do know. God said to me, 'Go from your country, your people and your father's household to the land I will show you. I will make you into a great nation, and I will bless you; I will make your name great and you will be a blessing. I will bless those who bless you, and whoever curses you I will curse; and all peoples on earth will be blessed through you' (Genesis 12:1-3 NIV). I didn't get all the instructions; I had no idea how God was going to do what He said. He told me I would be a great nation, even though I didn't have any children. On top of that, my wife was barren. If I would have sat down and tried to figure out how all of this would happen, I would have never left Haran. I chose to obey the command. He told me to go to a land that He would show me, so I left and trusted God to show me the path. Nicole, if you obey the Lord, you will receive your inheritance. God is a father who has an inheritance stored up for His children."

Suddenly, I woke up from my sleep. Had I just dreamed that I'd had a conversation with Abraham himself? It felt so real. I turned on the lamp next to my bed. The first thing I saw when I turned on the light was Lavender sitting on the edge of my bed, staring at me.

"Ahh! Lavender, why are you sitting on the edge of my bed?! That crept me out!"

"How is it that I am creeping you out when you have heavenly visitations so frequently?"

"I don't know. Maybe it's because you're a cat, and you all like to crouch and stare a lot."

"Oh, sorry. I often forget that humans don't like being stared at in the dark. But, I was just waiting for you to wake up so I could ask you what you learned from meeting Abraham."

"Well, I learned to trust God, and when I don't understand something, to keep on walking in obedience. He gave me fatherly advice. He reminded me of a father who wanted his kids to learn. It was practical advice that resonated within me. It was comforting because the father of faith said how he didn't know all the answers; he just trusted God."

Lavender pointed her paw towards the journal on my nightstand. I grabbed it, opened it and wrote:

Journal Entry 4/12/2019

Thank you for all that you have shown me. Thank you for showing me the proper way to live. You have shown me the life of Abraham and how he trusted you, even though he didn't have all the details. I want to be like Abraham and trust you without the details. I believe you are a rewarder of those who diligently seek you. I will follow the advice that Abraham gave me. No matter how impossible a situation looks, I will trust God in it. I will complete the task He has assigned to me. I want to receive all that God has for me. Lord, lead me like you led Abraham. Guide me like you guided Abraham.

Chapter 9

GROWTH AND JOURNEY

For a couple of days after my encounter with Abraham, I had not had any heavenly visitations. I assumed that I wasn't going to see anyone else. It was late in the afternoon, and I was cleaning out my closet. I had accumulated so many clothes from working at Stacie Pearl that my closet looked like a junky retail store. I turned on some upbeat music and started to de-clutter. As I sorted through the clothes, I threw everything that I was giving away on my bed for me to organize later. After everything was in order and I'd color-coordinated my wardrobe, I turned to the huge pile of clothes on the bed that needed to be donated to charity. I went into the kitchen to grab a couple of large paper bags to put the donations in.

As soon as I walked past the kitchen, I felt the room change. I knew that meant I had another heavenly visitation. I put the bags down and sat at the kitchen table. I knew that someone was going to come see me, and the kitchen table seemed to be the meeting place. Time had stopped, and it seemed as if I was waiting for-ever. I started to get up from the table when a flash of light blinded me. I closed my eyes and looked down. After a few seconds, the light fad-ed and I saw a man sitting across from me. His stature and poise were kingly.

The first king of Israel was a sight to behold. Everything about him looked noble. He was the epitome of a king. All I could do was stare at him. In that moment, I completely understood why God had chosen him to be king over Is-rael.

King Saul said to me, "God has given me the privilege to come into your space to share with you the lessons I learned in life. Take my words to heart and don't make the same mistakes I made while I was king of Israel. Be honest with yourself and confess to God your internal struggles. I was more concerned about what others thought of me than what God thought of me. I remember when Prophet Samuel had

given me the instructions of the Lord and I was
supposed to wait for Samuel to come to Gilgal
to offer the burnt offering. I was impatient and I
saw that my men were scattering in fear. I
should have prayed and asked the Lord to help
me obey the command He had given. Instead,
I offered the burnt offering myself. As soon as
I'd finished, I saw Samuel trekking up the hill.
In hindsight, that was when I should have
asked for forgiveness because I'd disobeyed
the Lord. However, when Samuel rebuked me,
I didn't apologize for disobeying God; instead, I
blamed everyone else. I even told Samuel that
I was compelled to offer the burnt offering because he was late in coming and my soldiers
were scattering. Instead of humbling myself, I
actually blamed the prophet. Don't live how I
lived. Read the Bible and learn from my mistakes. Let the Holy Spirit help you understand
each passage so that you can prosper in all
you do. Why wait until it's burnt up before you
finally see what you have lost? Hosea said it
best when he quoted God, saying, "My people

are destroyed from lack of knowledge" (Hosea 4:6/ NIV). In hindsight, I would have changed. If I only knew the truth, I would have done it differently. Had I known that there were consequences to my actions, I would have lived a better life. Who would have thought that the gift of kingship had to be maintained through obedience? Had I known offering the burnt offering would have cost me my throne, I would have obeyed God's instructions and waited for the Prophet Samuel. I let fear get the best of me and chose to do my own thing, instead of obeying the instructions God gave me. When Samuel was coming up the mountain and I was walking down to greet him, I felt a ping of regret. If I only knew he would have come at that time, I would not have offered up the burnt offering. If only I would have listened to God, instead of listening to my situation, things would be different. Nicole, don't wait until you're overtaken by the enemy in a besieged land to come to your senses. Come to your senses now! Listen with your heart now! The lust of the eyes is pointless and jealousy is vain. I remember after I died, I heard the lament of David, and I wept without tears. I mourned with my spirit. My life had ended before it's time. I let panic and fear consume me. When I was wounded by the archers, I was stricken with panic and didn't even think to pray to God. As I fell on my spear, regret and anguish overpowered me. My eyes had opened and all I could think of was what I'd done. In that moment of panic, I asked the Amalekite to do a foolish thing—to kill the Lord's anointed. The first king of Israel fell. How the mighty have fallen to such a weak enemy! Because jealousy and bitterness had occupied my heart, I lost the desire to serve God. When I lost the desire to serve God, I also lost my victory, for victory and success are only maintained by God. Learn from this king and hunger after the Living God. He is your only help. If you take your eyes off Him, you will live in regret like I did. Oh, how the mighty have fallen! Don't let those words be your anthem.

May you trust in the Lord. He will keep you victorious."

In all his kingly glory, King Saul stood up from the table. His words were like that of a loving father who wanted to make up for the past mistakes he'd made in his life. He stood by the entrance of light and turned back to look at me. "Trust in the Lord with all your heart and lean not on your own understanding" (Proverbs 3:5/ NIV).

Without saying another word, he turned back to the door of light and he was gone. I had to slowly take in all that King Saul said. His words penetrated my spirit. I felt every word he'd spoken. All the heavenly encounters I had were profound, but meeting King Saul was different. He truly wanted me to learn from his life.

While I sat at the table replaying everything King Saul said in my head, Lavender nudged my leg with her head.

"So, you got to meet the first king of Israel. What did you learn?"

I marveled. "He told me profound things; he gave me the treasures of the wise. He told me about the wickedness of jealousy and rejection and the deep heaviness of regret. His message was the most encouraging because he was adamant about telling me how to not let rejection ruin my life. Saul's advice even gave me insight into how the evil spirit had tried to turn me away from serving God. It was rejection that the evil spirit was using to get me to see God in a bad light. The evil spirit tried to use the rejection from failed relationships to get me to stop serving God. Now I understand why Saul warned me about being consumed by jealousy and rejection. If I become consumed by those things, I can't live for God."

Lavender meowed and then said, "Open your Bible and see how he lived. Read about his life first. Afterwards, take his advice and learn from his mistakes."

I nodded in agreement and then opened my Bible to 1 Samuel 9 and began to read about King Saul.

Chapter 10

RAISED TO LIFE

It was a new day and Lavender was doing her usual morning routine, circling my legs until I let her outside onto the patio. Even though she had been speaking to me, she was still a cat. After I let Lavender outside, I walked into the kitchen to get a hot cup of tea. I grabbed my tea, and then headed towards the patio to sit and enjoy the fresh air. Grey clouds covered the sky and it started to drizzle down rain while Lavender and I were sitting on the patio. The rain started coming down faster and with more force. Heavy rain started to beat down on the deck of the patio. I took a sip of tea, closed my eyes and took a deep breath. When I opened my eyes, I was on a boat.

Rain thrashed the boat. Someone yelled, "All hands on deck! The boat's about to break; lighten the load!" I could hardly see my hands in front of me. The sky was pitch black and rain was pounding down so hard that it stung my face. The ocean waves tossed the boat back and forth. I was afraid that the boat was going to break in half and sink. I grabbed onto a wooden box and tried to steady myself. The ship was too shaky and it was difficult to move. The harsh movements of the boat caused my head to ache and my stomach to churn. I wanted to vomit. I ended up sitting against a wooden crate while holding my stomach. I heard a man shout, "Cry out to your gods! We are about to die!" I heard chants, moans and groans. I even prayed with them. "Lord, save us!" I cried. I heard some commotion down by the deck. I peeked over the wooden crate to see what was happening. The lightning flash gave me a quick glimpse of what was happening.

From what I could see, a group of rain-soaked men looked like they were about to throw a man overboard. I leaned on the crate to get closer; this was so that whenever the lighting flashed again, I would be able to see better. I watched them grab the man. It was odd that the man didn't resist. "What is happening?" I thought to myself. We were all just praying. Now, they are throwing a man overboard. The boat began to violently shake, and I fell next to the crate I was leaning on. A strong wave beat against the side of the boat and it knocked me to the ground. The boat was slick from the heavy rainfall and I couldn't keep my footing. Once more, a wave pounded against the boat and before I had a chance to grab onto anything, I was swept into the sea.

I was engulfed in total darkness. The water pulled me deeper and deeper under its waves. I tried to swim, but I had no sense of direction and I was losing strength. The more I struggled against the current, the weaker I became. Finally, my strength gave way and I stopped moving. I no longer had the energy or will-power to fight. All I could hear was a slow heartbeat as I faded in an out of consciousness. In my mind I prayed, "Father, save me." Underneath the sea, I was tossed and hurled side-to-side by the water. My whole body was being thrashed around by water. I still was not fully conscious, but I soon realized that I was able to breathe. I smelled rotten fish, and the air was thick and damp. I couldn't see because it was pitch black, but I heard a constant pounding. *Thump thump thump.* It sounded like a heartbeat. "Am I dead; did I go to hell?" I thought to myself. Not too far from me, I heard a man quietly speaking. His voice was faint, but I heard him praying.

"In my distress I called to the Lord, and he answered me. From deep in the realm of the dead I called for help, and you listened to my cry. You hurled me into the depths, into the very heart of the seas, and the currents swirled about me; all your waves and breakers swept over me. I said, 'I have been banished from your sight; yet I will look again toward your holy temple.' The engulfing waters threatened me, the deep surrounded me; seaweed was wrapped around my head. To the roots of the mountains I sank down; the earth beneath barred me in forever. But you, Lord my God, brought my life up from the pit.

When my life was ebbing away, I remembered you, Lord, and my prayer rose to you, to your holy temple.

Those who cling to worthless idols turn away from God's love for them. But I, with shouts of grateful praise, will sacrifice to you. What I have vowed I will make good. I will say, 'Salvation comes from the Lord'" Jonah 2:2-9 (NIV).

At the close of the prayer, I opened my eyes. I was being washed onto a beach. It was dawn. I squinted at the sun rising in the East. I looked up at the sky while I laid on my back; the waves swept against my legs. Off to the side of me, I saw a man crawling towards the beach as the waves pushed him out of the sea. I looked over at him. There was seaweed wrapped around him and he looked like a zombie coming out of the sea. He seemed familiar to me, so much so that I felt comfortable calling out to him. "Hey, where are you going?!"

In a daze, he replied, "I'm going to Nineveh," as he staggered along. I felt compelled to follow him. I wobbled as I got my footing together and followed him. I stayed behind and followed him at a distance. I stepped into his footprints as we walked along. He started to talk. I wasn't sure if he was talking to me or to himself, but I listened closely.

Jonah uttered, "During despair, I thanked God for being my help and salvation. How could I praise in the bottom of the sea? How could I exalt Him in the belly of a beast? I was able to praise Him because I looked past the obvious and lifted my head towards His Holy Temple. I was in the heart of the sea and you heard my plea. You remembered me, even though I tried to forget you. While I was among the dead buried in the sea, I thanked you for being the only salvation. I will honor you and obey your commands. What I have vowed, I will make good. I will proclaim that salvation comes from the Lord. The mercy He extended to me, He will extend to Nineveh. I was dead in the belly of the sea, yet I was raised to life. I will go to Nineveh just as God said and raise that great city to life. I will speak forth the Word of Life, and I know they will live."

I looked down at the ground to be mindful of my footing. I realized the sandy ground I had been walking on had become a black track and my bare feet were suddenly in my workout shoes. I was at the high school track walking laps. I stopped and looked around. "Is this real?" I questioned myself. I saw kids playing flag football on the field and I saw a few people on the track jogging. I kept on walking around the track. Somehow, moving was helping me process what I'd just experienced. I'd just walked in the footsteps of the prophet Jonah from the famous Bible story of Jonah and the whale. I was there with him inside the whale's stomach and I witnessed God saving him. I even heard the prayer Jonah offered up before God commanded the whale to spit us out.

"That was incredible; this is real!" I blurted out loud. I looked around to make sure I hadn't startled anyone with my sudden outburst. Thankfully, no one heard or noticed me. I started to smile at the things that I had experienced. I was so excited that the Bible was becoming real to me—so real, in fact, that I got to experience the very things I'd read about in the Bible. I remember laying half dead in the stomach of the whale with seaweed and mucus wrapped around me. The quiet prayer of Jonah sounded like faint music; it soothed my mind and soul. I felt his words touch my spirit. They gave me hope to call on the name of the Lord. To be able to see and touch the very things I read about forever changed my life.

The journey started when I asked for the Holy Spirit. God answers prayers, so He'd given me what I'd asked for. I received the Holy Spirit and my life changed forever. I received supernatural Bible studies from my cat. I realized that Lavender was a tool God used to help me grow and mature as a Christian. Who would ever think that God would use a talking cat to help me get to know Him—especially a black cat? Most people have misguided beliefs about black cats. I guess Balaam never thought a talking donkey would save his life. I learned that you can't guess how God will save you. He has an infinite ways to answer prayers. I have tasted and seen that the Lord is good.

At the beginning of the year, I had no connection to the Bible. I didn't get it. I considered it as a history book, but as soon as I received the Holy Spirit, I was able to experience the Bible. I'm reminded of a passage of scripture in 1 Corinthians 2:14. It reads, "The person without the Spirit does not accept the things that come from the Spirit of God but considers them foolishness and cannot understand them because they are discerned only through the Spirit." When I received the Holy Spirit, I was able to see with my eyes the meaning inside the text. I no longer was bored with reading, but I was able to see myself in each chapter. I could relate to the people in the Bible and I could even apply the lessons learned to my everyday life. I feel like I've learned the secret to life.

A jewel was buried, and I found it—a treasure was hidden, but it was revealed to me. It's available to everyone who is looking. If you seek, you will find. If you search for God with a genuine heart, He will reveal himself to you. I found purpose when I received the Holy Spirit. My life changed for the better.

Months passed and Spring was in full effect. Texas's wildflowers popped up overnight— Bluebonnets, Buttercups and Indian Paintbrushes covered the fields. The sweet aroma of Spring was in the air. The warm breeze felt inviting.

One day, while sipping tea out on the patio, I asked Lavender, "How am I supposed to apply everything I've learned this year to my everyday life now? What do I do now? I will go back to work tomorrow."

Lavender answered, "What do you mean? Just go to work and do your job."

"Yes. Naturally, but now that I have had these experiences with people in the Bible, what am I supposed to do with all this information?"

"Nicole, what you have is a revelation. Use the revelation you have received to help other people. The store you work at has lots of people who have issues and problems. You can be a light in their lives. Did you forget that you are the light of the world?"

"I just don't want to come off as being spooky."

"Well, I'm not telling you to scream what you have encountered on the mountaintops. If you did that, they would think you've lost your mind."

I laughed at Lavender's catty response. She was right. Telling people probably wasn't the best idea. However, I can give them some advice to help them.

"Hey Vendy, do you want to help me pick out an outfit for work tomorrow?"

Lavender hissed, "No thanks. I want to bask in the sun a little longer."

I laughed to myself and said, "You're such a cat."

I stepped into my closet and looked around at my massive wardrobe. Instead of picking out my outfit for work, I felt led to pray.

"Lord, help me to not waste the experiences you gave me. Let me be used by you to change lives. Let me be an answer to some-one's prayer. This is the place you want me to be so let me be a light to help lead people to you. Give me wisdom to say the right words. Thank you for all you have done in my life."

To be honest, I was a little excited about going back to work. I missed the customers and all their interesting behaviors. Plus, I missed my coworkers—some of them had called and texted me during my month-long furlough, but it wasn't the same as seeing them. My first day back at work from my month-long vacation was great. Everyone was happy to see me, and I even got a welcome back cake. The greatest news of all was that Diva was getting married and moving to Arizona. We all noticed a huge difference in her personality. I suppose everyone is nicer when they are in love.

As the months flew by, many things changed. When Diva left, I was promoted to store manager and I was able to attend workshops at the London corporate office. My life had completely changed. I always made a point to find a story in the Bible that related to what was going on in my life. The Holy Spirit helped me to understand what I am reading so much so that the Bible became relevant to my life. If I had an issue, I could find the solution in the Bible.

The Summer of 2019 flew by. All I could remember was that tie-dye was trending and it looked like the late 60's had exploded in Stacie

Pearl. I wore a tie-dye scarf as a hair tie to embrace the Summer trend, but I didn't go overboard with it. When I got home that day, I noticed that Lavender was still napping on the couch. "Hey Vendy, do you want to know how my day was?" She meowed. After this, she did a cute little cat-stretch before hopping off the couch to rub my leg.

"Why are you meowing and not talking?"
Lavender looked up at me and meowed again.
"Oh no. Last time you stopped talking, some weird stuff happened."
That whole day, I was on my guard, ready to rebuke and cast out any evil spirit that tried to run into my life. However, nothing happened; everything was normal.

As the days passed and the seasons changed, Lavender never spoke again. She was back to being a normal cat. I was a little sad that she hadn't forewarned me that she would stop talking. I had assumed that she would always be my talking cat. I suppose she completed her task, and God took away her ability to speak. She still has her quirky characteristics, and she still sits near when I read the Bible. Before she'd stopped talking, our last conversation had been about the Holy Spirit. She told me that the Holy Spirit is with me and would not leave me. She'd told me that the wisdom to make good decisions will always be present because I have put my trust in God.

I have spiritually matured these past few months. I remember hardly being able to stay awake when I read the Bible. Nowadays, I am so engrossed in it that I don't want to put it down. I used to think the Bible was a history book, but I now see it as a living book. It may sound odd, but the Bible is a book that can fix anyone's life. The people in the Bible had experiences that I could learn from. Initially, I hadn't thought of the people in the Bible as real people—only characters. Now that I have seen with my own eyes the stories in the Bible come to life, I have responded with a changed life-style. No longer did I live selfishly and serve only me, myself and I. Instead, I now do what God says I should do. What I have gone through is only the beginning. Receiving the Holy Spirit was only step one in my life-long journey of walking with God. I have a whole journey ahead of me. I am no longer unprepared. Instead, I am equipped and ready to live for God.

www.ingramcontent.com/pod-product-compliance
Lightning Source LLC
Chambersburg PA
CBHW060826120626
46557CB00001B/392